Tales From

Pillow Pets

Dreamland ™

The Secret Unicorn
of Engardia

Written by Eve & Brooke West

Illustrated by James Arrington

Published by Gooseworks

HX Printing, Guangzhou, China
May 2011   Batch 1

www.mypillowpets.com
www.hxbookprinting.com

ISBN: 978-0-615-48213-2

**To Special Friends
David and Lynn**

Pillow Pets Dreamland is a magical place full of adventure and fun! So close your eyes and let your dreams take you there. In Dreamland there is a beautiful land called Engardia. As you fly through the clouds, you will see a charming village. Then, upon landing, you will find yourself in front of a castle, with magical golden gates.

However, you must know that the Engardian castle is guarded by a fierce, angry dragon.

After taking a brief walk through the woods you will find yourself at Pokey Pond, where Ms. Lady Bug and Buzzing Bumble Bee are lying on their backs in fits of laughter. You see, Friendly Frog is telling them a funny story.

Pokey Pond is shaped like a star, and when the sun shines down upon it, it sparkles like a giant diamond.

Ms. Lady Bug and Buzzing Bumble Bee were crying with laughter, so much so that they had woken up Puffy Duck. He swam over. "Quack quack," he greeted them, his eyes wide with excitement.

"Hello, Puffy Duck," said Friendly Frog, as he jumped off of his lily pad.

"What shall we do today?" Ms. Lady Bug asked them.

"Well," said Friendly Frog, "Sir Horse is back with his family and Magical Unicorn will be waiting for him. I have always wanted to see if she is as beautiful as she is rumored to be."

Sir Horse is a magnificent horse who often travels to Engardia. On one of his visits, he made friends with what was thought to be a village myth...Magical Unicorn. She lives in the castle, and the dragon forbids her to leave. She only ever escapes to see Sir Horse.

"We should definitely try to find her," said Ms. Lady Bug.
"Come on, gang!" With that, they headed towards the castle,
Puffy Duck trying to keep up as he waddled clumsily along.

They made their way to the village square. "I'm sooo hungry," Buzzing Bumble Bee grumbled.

"You're always hungry, Buzzing!" giggled Ms. Lady Bug.

After wandering through the village for some time, they finally reached the castle and stood in front of its high walls. "Quack, how will we get in there?" said Puffy Duck.

Friendly Frog knew just what to do. He stretched out his legs, squeezed his hands into the castle's cracks, and — becoming spider-like — climbed all the way to the top where he found a small window that he managed to climb through.

"Oh boy, here he goes again," Ms. Lady Bug muttered.

Friendly Frog had made it inside! Nervously, he hopped along the west wing's corridors, looking to find Magical Unicorn. He was worried that the dragon would spot him. Upon reaching the end of the corridor, he found himself standing in front of a very large mirror.

While smiling at his own reflection, he noticed a long piece of yellow string attached to a hatch. With a quick tug, the hatch opened, and he fell down into a deep, dark hole!

Friendly Frog's fall was cushioned by a stack of golden hay. As he bounced his way to the floor, he looked up to find that the myth he'd heard so much about was REAL – there in front of him stood the most beautiful creature he had ever seen...

MAGICAL UNICORN!

Friendly Frog grinned nervously. Magical Unicorn's large blu
eyes lit up with what seemed like a smile, and she moved
her head in a way that shook her whole mane. Friendly Frog
suggested to her that she come with him to meet the rest o
the group. She looked nervous, and confessed to Friendly
Frog that she didn't fit in with the other animals.

"My friends would never judge you," he reassured her.

She smiled at Friendly Frog's confidence. "Okay, I'll come with you, and you can wait with me to meet Sir Horse... but the Dragon must not know that I have left."

Friendly Frog smiled back, and with that, they both quietly left the room.

While creeping slowly through the castle corridors, they could hear the fierce dragon sleeping. It snored so loudly that it made the whole castle tremble. Then, just as they reached the back door, the castle halls went quiet. Friendly Frog looked at Magical Unicorn just as they heard a feirce ROAR!

"Hurry this way," Magical Unicorn whispered.

Quickly, she opened the back door with her horn. Friendly Frog then hopped outside as fast as his little frog legs could carry him. Magical Unicorn followed him outside and together they ran to the edge of the village to wait for Sir Horse to return.

Meanwhile, it was becoming late.

Ms. Lady Bug and Buzzing Bumble Bee had grown tired of waiting, so after leaving Puffy Duck at Pokey Pond, they headed back to the castle to find Friendly Frog.

"Ms. Lady Bug, I better not be in trouble – it's getting dark!" Buzzing muttered.

"We must go, Buzzing. We need to make sure Friendly Frog is safe," Ms. Lady Bug insisted.

Upon arriving at the castle, they could hear the dragon roaring with anger. Then, out of nowhere, a dragonfly appeared, dressed in a black coat. "Hello," he whispered, hovering next to Ms. Lady Bug, "are you looking for your friend?"

"Yes, we are. He's a frog about this tall." Ms. Lady Bug held her hand above the ground.

"Oh, I know him; he left with that stunning unicorn. That's why the dragon is so angry. Go to the end of the village; you will find them there."

"Well, thank you – we must be off!" said Buzzing Bumble Bee politely. With that, they turned their backs on him and flew away.

As they arrived, they could see the silhouettes of Magical Unicorn and Friendly Frog who were sitting with their backs toward them. Ms. Lady Bug and Buzzing Bumble Bee flew over to join them.

"Hi!" they said together.

Friendly Frog began to introduce them.

Far away in the distance, they could see a cloud of dust. Then, Suddenly Sir Horse came galloping in. He looked so radiant as he trotted over to the fence. Sir Horse moved his head, urging Magical Unicorn to follow him. She did so, and quickly smiled at the group, as if to say, "Thank you."

Sir Horse and Magical Unicorn galloped away into the open fields toward the Great Mountains. They soon met up with Sir Horse's family who were busy planning their next great adventure. As they greeted her, she smiled,

As the sun began to set Sir Horse and Magical Unicorn splashed and played in a nearby stream while his family talked of the fun they would have. The horses' adventures were always exciting, especially this one. They were on their way to an enchanted forest where Sir Horse's Granddad was living. He was a wise horse who had once lived in Engardia.

As the stars shone brightly, Sir Horse's mother and father stood alone, discussing which direction to take.

Magical Unicorn and Sir Horse looked up into the night sky. A shooting star streaked by, it's tail sparkling with shimmery dust.

"Make a wish," Sir Horse whispered.

Magical Unicorn smiled and closed her eyes tight: "I just did."

The two trotted over to Sir Horse's parents. As they approached them, Sir Horse turned to Magical Unicorn.

"You *will* come with us, won't you?"

Feeling unsure, Magical Unicorn nodded her head shyly.

"We will leave tomorrow at sunrise," Sir Horse's mother said.

"You two get some rest tonight. It will be a long journey, and we don't know when or if we will return," Sir Horse's father added.

A frightened look came across Magical Unicorn's face as she took a deep breath.

The pair found a spot under a large oak tree to rest.

Magical Unicorn tried to sleep, but just couldn't keep her eyes shut. After an hour, she woke Sir Horse.

"Wake up." She nudged him with her horn.

"What's wrong?" he inquired sleepily.

"I shouldn't be going with you!," she said uneasily.

She explained how she felt, hoping Sir Horse would understand.

After listening, he smiled. "I'll take you back to the village now, before the others wake."

With that, they began their journey back to Engardia.

"Do you know what my wish was?" Magical Unicorn said as they galloped along, the sun now high in the sky. "It was that I would feel confident enough to be myself. I realize now that I should love who I am."

Sir Horse was so happy, "Yes, you should!"

Sir Horse walked her
back to the fence.

"Magical Unicorn, You should be proud of
who you are."

She smiled, and they rubbed noses affectionately. Magical
Unicorn's horn lit up, and a rainbow appeared in the sky. With
that, she took to the air and headed toward the village.

Magical Unicorn's mane was sparkling as she flew, leaving a trail of pink dust behind her.

Every Pillow Pet in the village looked up to the sky in amazement.

Magical Unicorn reached the star-shaped pond, which until then she had only heard stories of.

Friendly Frog sat on his lily pad as Puffy Duck, Ms. Lady Bug, and Buzzing Bumble Bee sat nearby, dangling their feet into the water. Friendly Frog looked down into the palm of his hand, and noticed pink stardust. As he looked up, so did the rest of the animals. It was Magical Unicorn!

Ms. Lady Bug was so excited to see Magical Unicorn that she flew over to her and kissed her on the cheek. Friendly Frog then jumped off of his lily pad and showed Magical Unicorn to a spot under the willow tree.

"This is your home now," he said kindly.

Magical Unicorn joined in the laughter as they all sat by the pond, enjoying another beautiful day in Engardia.

The End.